Fool's

Sir JonTonio

First Edition published by 2024

Copyright © 2024 by Sir JonTonio

All rights reserved. No part of this publication may be

reproduced, stored or transmitted in any form or by any means, electronic, mechanical, photocopying, recording, scanning, or otherwise without written permission from the publisher. It is

illegal to copy this book, post it to a website, or distribute it by any other means without permission.

This novel is entirely a work of fiction. The names, characters and incidents portrayed in it are the work of the author's

imagination. Any resemblance to actual persons, living or dead, events or localities is entirely coincidental.

Sir JonTonio asserts the moral right to be identified as the author of this work.

Sir JonTonio has no responsibility for the persistence or accuracy of URLs for external or third-party Internet Websites referred to

in this publication and does not guarantee that any content on such Websites is, or will remain, accurate or appropriate.

Designations used by companies to distinguish their products are often claimed as trademarks. All brand names and product names used in this book and on its cover are trade names, service marks, trademarks and registered trademarks of their respective owners.

The publishers and the book are not associated with any product or vendor mentioned in this book. None of the companies

referenced within the book have endorsed the book.

First Edition

I want to dedicate this book to my children...let this be an example that you can do anything you put your mind to. I love you, Tay and Kam.

*I want to dedicate this book to my father and my aunts.
May y'all rest in peace.*

Table of contents

- Balancing Acts
  - The Art of Conversation
- Vibes and Tensions
- A Quiet Escape
- Sisterhood and Secrets
- Morning After and Wedding Bells
- Calls and Commitments
- Bridging Paths and New Beginnings
- Crew Love and Pre-Wedding Banter
- Heartfelt Promises
- The Vows of Love and Faith
- Embracing Vulnerability
- My Sister's Keeper
- Unexpected Connections
- The Test of Loyalty
- Skeletons
- Notes

Acknowledgment

Greetings everyone,

I am thrilled to share this moment with you all. First and foremost, I'd like to extend my heartfelt thanks to everyone who has supported me throughout my journey. I understand that this journey has been long and often stressful, but your unwavering support has kept me going. As I write this, please know how truly grateful I am for the conversations, car rides, hugs, prayers, and tough love you've given me. Becoming an author is something I never imagined; I knew I could tell a story but crafting a narrative over many pages is a remarkable achievement.

Words cannot express my gratitude for all the experiences we've shared, but know that I love you all, and the future only gets brighter from here.

Now, onto the acknowledgments. This part isn't hard, but I don't want to miss anyone's name, as many have played crucial roles in my journey.

Firstly, thanks to God, the head of my life. Truly, without God's guidance, I wouldn't be here today sharing my gratitude, humor, and imagination. I encourage everyone not to be afraid to pursue what God shows you. In 2017, God gave me a dream that revealed I would create something that would generate multiple streams of revenue, not just for me and my family, but also for others. This is a testament to the power of getting out of your own way and trusting God.

Secondly, I want to give special thanks to the incredible women in my life who have been there since the very beginning. Momma and Maw Maw, I love you both immensely. Because of you, I am the strong black man I am today. You've supported me through my lowest points without judgment. Your resilience through challenges—from the house fire on Camp Street to Hurricane Katrina, surgeries, and overcoming breast cancer—has shown me that God's presence is ever-lasting. Your strength to endure and still smile is truly admirable. A mother's love is unmatched, and I publicly express my deepest love and gratitude for both of you.

To all my siblings, I love you, and you know what's up when I come home!

Special shoutouts go to:

- *The Butlers*
- *The Griffins*
- *Ms. Terrika Bell*
- *The Nelsons*
- *Chef Trizzy*
- *Charley Whop*
- *T.G.F. (Tru Gorrilla Family)*
- *My church family*
- *And everyone else who has supported me*

If I didn't mention your name, please know it's a lapse of memory, not of heart. Thank you all once again.

Preface

Fool's Gold is about a group of people whose are intertwined in the most complex but nurturing way.
Relationships will be tried through and through; friendships will endure the ultimate test. This series will have you at the edge of your seat, biting your nails, intrigued craving for more. You will see if love really conquers all, or if it's just a word to be thrown around.

WARNING!!! Everything is not what it always appears to be.

"Love isn't something you find. Love is something that finds you."

- LORETTA YOUNG

I was just a fool searching for gold Trying to find ways to fill my soul manipulating life to obtain goals Fear growing through life lonely and old Experiencing pain that turns my heart cold Internally timid with an exterior that's bold Taking responsibility for the things I control Can't trust everyone you meet because this here is FOOL'S GOLD.

Chapter 1

Balancing Acts

Antonio lay sprawled on his bed, staring at the ceiling, his thoughts consumed by Andrea. The gentle hum of the ceiling fan did little to distract him. The rhythmic whirl above seemed to mirror the chaos of his mind. Just as he was about to close his eyes, his phone buzzed on the nightstand. Glancing at the screen, a smile crept across his face.

"Hey, I was just thinking about you," Antonio said, answering the call.

"Oh really? What happened to you last night?" Andrea's voice was a mix of curiosity and disappointment.

"Last night?" Antonio replied, feigning ignorance.

"Umm yeah, that's what I said," Andrea retorted. "You were supposed to come over and meet my family like you promised."

"That was last night? I forgot. I was excited to meet them too," Antonio said, but his tone lacked conviction.

Andrea sucked her teeth, a clear sign of her annoyance. "Stop lying. You weren't trying to meet my family, or you would have."

"Nah, for real, you know I wanted to meet your sexy momma. Tell her thank you for me," Antonio said, attempting to lighten the mood.

"Thank you? What are you talking about, Tonio?" Andrea's voice was laced with confusion.

SIR JONTONIO

"I want to thank her for sharing her blessing with me. I'm sorry, bae," Antonio said softly.

Andrea cleared her throat, her silence making Antonio uneasy. He waited, holding his breath.

"Aww. You're so sweet, and you truly have the gift of gab. But I'm still mad at you," she said, sucking her teeth again.

Antonio forced a laugh. "There you go again, tryna tell me about my gifts."

"Tonio, stop. Ain't nobody tryna preach. I'm just saying you're smooth and can talk your way out of anything," Andrea said.

"I'm tryna talk my way into dem drawls," Antonio quipped.

Andrea laughed. "You so nasty. Plus, you know you're not ready for this."

Laughing, Antonio said, "You must like sounding tough because we both know you're the one that's not ready. My lil virgin."

"Tonio, don't do that. You know I'm saving myself for marriage," Andrea said, her tone serious.

"Yeah, I know, bae. I was just playing. You know you keep me on the right track. Well, look, I have to go. I'll see you later, okay?" Antonio said.

"Okay, boo. Are you coming to church on Friday? I would love it if you came," Andrea said.

"I don't..." Antonio began, but Andrea quickly interjected.

"Please, please, please, please," she pleaded.

"Okay, okay, okay, you got it, love. I'll be there. Bye," Antonio said, relenting.

"No, don't say bye. Byes are forever. We're in this till the wheels fall off," Andrea insisted.

"Bae, I gotta go," Antonio said, chuckling.

"Say it," Andrea demanded.

"Say what?" Antonio asked.

"Say it," Andrea repeated.

FOOL'S GOLD

"You're beautiful, you're amazing, you're fearfully and wonderfully made, and I will conduct myself as a king to build up my empire that will be fitted for you, my Queen. I'll see you later," Antonio said, smiling.

"Aww, thank you. See you later, babe," Andrea said, and they disconnected the call.

Antonio placed his phone on his chest, staring back at the ceiling. His mind wandered to the first time he met Andrea. It was at a mutual friend's birthday party, and he was instantly captivated by her infectious laugh and the way she moved with such grace and confidence. They had spent the entire evening talking, sharing stories, and laughing until the early hours of the morning. He remembered the way her eyes sparkled when she talked about her dreams and ambitions, and he knew then that he wanted to be a part of her world.

He sighed, rolling over to his side, his fingers tracing the edges of the phone. The memory of last night's missed opportunity gnawed at him. He had genuinely been excited to meet Andrea's family, but a last-minute call from his brother needing help with a broken-down car had derailed his plans. He had intended to call Andrea and explain, but time slipped away, and before he knew it, the night was over.

His thoughts were interrupted by a knock on his bedroom door. "Antonio, I hope you're in there getting ready," his brother from another mother called out.

"Coming, bro. I'm getting ready now," he replied, swinging his legs over the side of the bed. He stood up, stretching his arms above his head, and started to get dressed.

Chapter 2

The Art of Conversation

Antonio got up and began to dress, preparing for his best friend Zeke's wedding. As he fastened his tie, his friend Brandon burst into the room, urging him to hurry. "That's what I'm doing," Antonio said, rolling his eyes. The two of them began reminiscing about the party they attended the previous night.

"Man, I can't believe how last night went," Antonio mused aloud.

"Bro, we were supposed to be out of there," Brandon said.

"I'm coming. Stop being a little broad," Antonio retorted.

"A little broad? Boy, I know you ain't talking. It's taking you 100 years to get dressed just like a female. You know it's a big day for Zeke today," Brandon said.

"I know. My dude finally tying the knot. Bruh, I'm glad he got everything outta his system last night. Bro was trippin' hard," Antonio said.

"Trippin'? Shoot, that man got to enjoy his last night as a free man, and plus, I know you ain't talking," Brandon shot back.

"What's that supposed to mean?" Antonio asked, raising an eyebrow.

"Bro, you had about three to five different women running all over the place talking 'bout Tonio is so fine, Tonio knows how to treat a lady, Tonio this, and Tonio that," Brandon said, laughing.

"Sounds like someone is salty when they should have been taking notes. How many times do I have to tell you? Conversation rules the nation. Once you figure that out and master it, you can't go wrong," Antonio declared, leaning back in his chair with a confident grin.

Brandon rolled his eyes, a hint of a smile playing on his lips. "Here you go again with your philosophy. Please, oh wise one, break it down for me and teach me."

Antonio laughed, the sound filling the room. "Bro, if you can spark a conversation and keep it flowing, you've got the keys to the kingdom. It's all about connecting, making the other person feel seen and heard. Take, for instance, that girl with the dimples and the coke bottle shape."

"Who? The one in pink or the one in red?" Brandon interrupted, leaning forward with interest.

"The one in pink," Antonio clarified, his eyes lighting up as he remembered. "When she first came in, she acted like she was too good to be approached by anyone. She was shooting you fools down left and right."

"Who? She didn't shoot me down. I saw she was acting all stuck-up, so I didn't say anything. You know how I am. I would have blown her off," Brandon retorted, crossing his arms defensively.

With a smirk, Antonio said, "Don't front. You were checking her out from the moment she walked in. You were scared to approach her because you didn't have confidence in your game. You felt like she was out of your league."

Brandon laughed, shaking his head. "Out of my league? That's not possible," he said, though his tone betrayed a hint of uncertainty.

"Really? Be honest. I'm not saying you don't get girls—I know you do. I've seen you in action. But last night, you froze up and went for the easier option. Bet you didn't even realize she was checking you out until you started drinking and smoking with the other girl," Antonio countered, his voice unwavering.

"Tell me you're lying! Something told me to go speak to her, but by the time I came around, you were all over it like white on rice on a paper plate in a snowstorm," Brandon exclaimed, his frustration evident.

FOOL'S GOLD

"Nah, I was just chilling, and she came up to me, asking where she knew me from," Antonio explained, shrugging nonchalantly.

"So, you already knew her?" Brandon asked, surprised.

"No, I didn't know her, but we've seen each other a few times at the club and at parties around campus," Antonio replied, his voice calm and collected.

"Okay, okay. So, what happened? Did you get her number?" Brandon inquired; his curiosity piqued.

"After I told her we didn't know each other, I introduced myself, and she told me her name. From there, I just asked if she was enjoying herself," Antonio recounted, his eyes twinkling with amusement. "We talked about the music, the drinks, and even the people at the party. She was impressed that I could keep the conversation going without any awkward pauses."

Brandon leaned back, contemplating Antonio's words. "So, it's all about keeping the conversation flowing, huh?" he mused.

"Exactly," Antonio affirmed. "And it's not just about talking; it's about listening too. People love to talk about themselves, their interests, their experiences. Ask the right questions, show genuine interest, and you'll have them eating out of your hand."

Brandon nodded slowly, a thoughtful expression on his face. "Alright, I get that. But what if you run out of things to say?"

"That's the beauty of it," Antonio said with a grin. "You don't have to do all the talking. Just steer the conversation in a direction where they feel comfortable sharing. And if you do run out of things to say, there's always humor. A good joke or a funny story can break the ice and keep things light."

"Man, you make it sound so easy," Brandon said, a hint of envy in his voice.

"It takes practice, just like anything else," Antonio replied. "But once you get the hang of it, you'll see how powerful it is. You'll be able to connect with anyone, anywhere. Trust me, it's a game-changer."

SIR JONTONIO

Brandon sighed, his mind racing with thoughts. "Alright, I'll give it a try. Next time, I won't just stand there like a deer in headlights."

"That's the spirit," Antonio said, clapping Brandon on the back. "And remember, confidence is key. Believe in yourself, and others will too."

They sat in silence for a moment, each lost in their thoughts. Finally, Brandon broke the silence. "So, did you end up getting her number?"

Antonio chuckled. "Yeah, I did. And we're going out this weekend."

Brandon shook his head, a smile spreading across his face. "You really are something else, man."

Antonio just shrugged, his grin widening. "Don't hate the player, just admire the game."

With their conversation concluded and Antonio finally dressed, they headed out the door, ready to celebrate Zeke's monumental day.

Chapter 3

Vibes and Tensions

Loud music pulsed in the background as Tori walked in with her friends, instantly becoming the center of attention. Guys tripped over themselves trying to catch her eye, but she brushed them off, her focus solely on Brandon—until she saw him flirting with other girls. Shifting her attention, she spotted Antonio and decided to approach him instead.

"Whew, I'm having a good time despite these lames offering me drinks every ten minutes," Tori complained.

Laughing, Antonio teased, "Why do you call them lames?"

"Because the moment I walked in, I felt the desperation in the air," Tori replied.

"So, you come to a party and don't want anyone to speak to you? Where do they do that at?" Antonio joked.

"No, it's not that. I had my eye on someone, and I could tell he noticed me too. We even made eye contact, but then he turned to talk to another girl," she said, playing with her hair for emphasis.

"Wait, wait... So, you played with your hair like you're in middle school or some romance movie?" Antonio laughed.

"Yes! But he didn't notice because those girls were all over him," Tori said, rolling her eyes.

"Why didn't you go up to him and say something?" Antonio asked.

"Who, me? I would never walk up to a guy," Tori declared firmly.

SIR JONTONIO

"Stop pretending. You can't say you'll never approach a guy and then come up to me to start a whole conversation," Antonio said.

"That's different! Hold on, did you just say I was being slick? How?" Tori demanded.

"Yeah, you walked over here asking if you know me, knowing well that you don't," Antonio pointed out.

"I thought I recognized you. Your face seemed familiar," Tori insisted.

"Uh-huh, but you did look familiar too. I was trying to figure out where I'd seen you, then you mentioned some parties we both attended. You weren't as stuck up then," Antonio remarked.

Laughing, Tori said, "I'm never stuck up."

"Says the one who shot everyone down and then came over to me," Antonio teased.

"If you think what those guys did counts as shooting their shot, it takes more than just offering me a drink and cheesy pick-up lines," Tori retorted.

"All girls say that. I don't believe it takes that much," Antonio mused.

"Oh, really? So, what does it take?" Tori asked, intrigued.

"Just being yourself usually works. For example, I didn't approach or signal for you to come talk to me—you did that on your own," Antonio said confidently.

Laughing, Tori responded, "You're silly. I came over to ask about your promotion and photography rates. You're not even my type."

"That was smooth. I like how quick you are on your feet," Antonio commented, impressed.

Visibly annoyed, Tori said, "There's nothing smooth about it. Don't flatter yourself. No one wants you. You're cute but not that cute."

As Tori started to walk away, Antonio gently grabbed her arm, pulling her back. "Wait, wait. I'm sorry. I assumed you were interested in me. I was just trying to feel you out," he explained.

FOOL'S GOLD

"Feel me out? I don't play games. I'm direct. If I wanted to talk to you, I would have said something," Tori snapped.

"Just like you did with my friend. You played with your hair and smiled," Antonio countered.

Tori admitted, "Okay, I thought he was cute, but I wouldn't approach him. Plus, he was busy with all those girls."

"But you came here while I was dancing and having a good time too. What's the difference?" Antonio questioned.

"You knew how to step away after a while. You were just chilling and vibing out," Tori explained.

"That's me. Laid-back, enjoying the vibe," Antonio said.

As a slow song began to play, Tori exclaimed, "That's my song. You don't seem like the type to like slow jams."

Laughing, Antonio replied, "Really? I'll show you." He grabbed her hand and led her to the dance floor.

"What are you trying to do?" Tori asked, following him.

"Dance. Stop talking and vibe out," Antonio said.

They danced for several songs, smiling and enjoying each other's company.

"You're pretty light on your feet. And you have rhythm," Tori noted.

Laughing, Antonio said, "A little? You're not bad yourself. Let's get a drink."

As they headed towards the kitchen, a guy holding a drink bumped into Tori, spilling it on her shirt. She pushed him back, and they began arguing.

"Damn, are you blind?! You spilled your drink on me!" Tori shouted.

"Damn hoe, you wasted my drink. Learn some manners!" the drunk guy retorted.

"Who are you calling a hoe?" Tori yelled back.

"Watch your mouth. Disrespecting her in my presence isn't a good look," Antonio warned, stepping in.

SIR JONTONIO

The drunk guy laughed and flashed a gun. But Antonio swiftly reached for his own gun. At that moment, the drunk guy's friend intervened, whispering urgently to calm the situation. Once things de-escalated, Tori sighed. "I have to go home and change. I can't stay like this."

Antonio looked at her shirt and said, "You don't have to leave. Take my shirt. I'm not ready for you to go yet. I'll turn around so you can change."

Laughing, Tori accepted. "Okay, but no peeking."

"I just protected your dignity. How would I look if I disrespected you now?" Antonio replied.

"Thank you," Tori said, genuinely impressed as she took his shirt.

Later, talking to his friend Brandon, Antonio recounted the story.

"So, does she have twin peaks or twin mosquito bites?" Brandon joked.

"I don't know, bro. I respected her wishes and didn't peek," Antonio said, laughing.

"Stop lying. I know you peeked. I would have peeked like grandma at church," Brandon teased.

"Bro, I gave her the drink and fifty dollars..." Antonio began, continuing the story.

Chapter 4

A Quiet Escape

"Here you go," Antonio said, handing Tori a drink.

"Thank you. What is this? Because I don't..." Tori started to say, but Antonio cut her off.

"It's Henny. I know you don't drink clear liquor, so I got this for you," Antonio replied.

"How do you know I don't drink clear?" Tori asked.

Jokingly, Antonio responded, "Because you don't look like the type."

"Don't look like the type? How do people who drink clear look?" Tori inquired; her curiosity piqued.

Laughing, Antonio said, "I'm just playing. See what it's like to be judged? Doesn't feel good, huh?"

Tori laughed and playfully hit Antonio on the shoulder. "You play too much. But seriously, how did you know, or did you just guess?"

"If there're too many options, just go with Henny," Antonio said with a grin.

Tori chuckled. "That was cute."

"Well, thank you. But honestly, I saw you turning down all those other drinks. So, I figured you'd prefer Henny," Antonio explained.

"How did you see all of that when you were dancing with that girl over there?" Tori asked, raising an eyebrow.

SIR JONTONIO

"I always keep an eye on things. Plus, the way you were ignoring those guys, I knew it wouldn't be long before you'd want to be in the company of a real man," Antonio said confidently.

"I guess so. Thanks for the drink," Tori said, taking a sip and savoring the flavor of the Hennessy.

The music grew louder, making it hard to hear. They looked at each other quizzically.

"What did you say? I can't hear you," Antonio shouted over the noise.

Tori leaned closer to him. "I said thank you for the drink. It's loud in here."

"Let's go somewhere quieter and talk," Antonio suggested.

Tori glanced around, considering the scene before nodding. "Sure. Where's a quieter place?"

"Upstairs. Follow me," Antonio said, taking her hand. He led her through the crowded room, weaving through dancing bodies and loud conversations. As they approached the stairs, the noise began to fade into the background. Antonio glanced back to make sure Tori was still with him and shot her a reassuring smile. They ascended the staircase, their footsteps muffled by the plush carpet.

At the top, the atmosphere was markedly more serene. The thumping bass from below was now just a distant hum. Antonio guided Tori down a dimly lit hallway adorned with framed photographs and subtle decor, creating an intimate ambiance.

"Here we are," Antonio said, opening a door to a cozy yet stylish lounge area. A few candles flickered on a side table, casting warm, mellow light around the room. A large window overlooked the city, its skyline glittering like a sea of stars against the night sky. Tori stepped inside, instantly feeling a sense of calm wash over her. Antonio closed the door gently behind them.

"Wow, this is nice," Tori said, taking in the atmosphere. She walked over to the window and gazed out, momentarily entranced by the city's beauty.

"Yeah, it's my favorite spot in the house," Antonio admitted. "It's a great place to get away from all the chaos downstairs."

Tori turned to face him, her eyes reflecting the candlelight. "Thanks for bringing me here. This is much better."

Antonio moved to a small bar in the corner and grabbed a bottle of wine. "Would you like some wine to go with your Henny? Or maybe just some water?"

"What do you recommend?" Tori asked playfully.

"Well, since we're in a quieter setting now, a nice glass of wine to sip might be good," Antonio suggested.

"Alright, you've convinced me," Tori said, smiling.

Antonio poured two glasses of a rich red wine and handed one to Tori. They clinked glasses gently and took a sip, savoring the smooth, velvety taste.

"So, tell me about yourself, Tori. I feel like we've crossed paths a few times, but never really had the chance to talk," Antonio said, taking a seat on a plush loveseat.

Tori joined him, tucking her legs beneath her. "Well, what do you want to know?" she asked, her eyes dancing with curiosity.

"Anything and everything. What keeps you busy? What are you passionate about?" Antonio asked, genuinely interested.

Tori took a moment to think. "Well, I'm really into photography. I love capturing moments, emotions, and stories through my lens. It's kind of my escape, you know?"

"That's amazing," Antonio said, impressed. "Do you have any favorite subjects or places you like to shoot?"

"I love nature, but I also enjoy street photography. There are so many stories hidden in the hustle and bustle of the city. Everyone has a story, and sometimes a single photograph can tell it all," Tori explained, her eyes lighting up as she spoke.

Antonio listened intently, nodding. "I'd love to see some of your work someday."

"I'd like that," Tori said, feeling warmth spread through her at his genuine interest.

"Thank you once again. You didn't have to do that downstairs," Tori said.

"No problem, and I couldn't let no—he stopped to laugh—Bantay Boy mess up our good time that we're having," Antonio said.

Tori laughed. "Plus, I couldn't let you walk around the party looking all ratchet with a wet shirt. Me and my bros would have been ribbing you."

"First of all, I'm not ratchet, and second of all, you and your lame bros would have got snapped on," Tori said.

"Whatever," Antonio said. "So, can I ask you a question?"

"Sure, what's up?" Tori said.

"Why did you want to come up here?" Antonio asked.

"Because I wanted to get to know you better and I wanted all of your attention," Tori said.

"Know me? And you had my attention already," Antonio said.

"Get on a more personal level and it was too loud down there. Plus, I didn't want another drunk fool to come bumping into you again. And then you would have turned into a shotta and set it off in this piece," Antonio said, laughing.

"I hear you. And you're not funny either. So, what made you come to the party?" Tori asked.

"All the females and liquor," Antonio said, laughing. Then added, "Nah, for real, it's my bro's bachelor party. I'm Zeke's best man. What brings you here?" Antonio asked.

Tori tried to avoid the question and said, "Dang that Henny got me feeling hot. You don't mind if I take my shirt off do you?"

FOOL'S GOLD

"You mean my shirt? Nah, it's cool. Get comfortable." Antonio sat on the bed. "You did not answer my question."

"Oh, my bad. My homegirls told me about it and told me I should come and have a couple of drinks, have fun, and maybe snag the right guy," Tori said.

"Snag the right guy?" Antonio said, Tori making up something to cover her tracks.

"Yeah, I have been having bad luck with meeting guys who are in relationships and use me for my body and play with my heart," Tori said.

Antonio looked away, thinking about Andrea. "Dang, that's messed up love. Well, at least you accomplished some of your goals for tonight," Antonio said.

"Oh, yeah? What did I accomplish, good sir?" Tori asked.

"You had drinks, danced, had fun, and got out of the house. And even..." Antonio started to say but Tori interrupted.

"Let me guess, and snagged the right guy?" Tori said.

"I was gonna say, even got to relieve some stress by bucking on a drunk fool," Antonio said, laughing.

"Oh, true. Well, you're right. I did accomplish my goals," Tori said.

"So, let me ask you a question now. Why did you come upstairs with me?" Antonio asked.

Tori sat down next to Antonio and grabbed his face. "Because when you stood up to that Bantay Boy downstairs I knew that I snagged the right guy." Tori said and kissed Antonio. They continued to talk, sharing stories, dreams, and laughter as the night stretched on. The connection between them grew, no longer just a fleeting encounter at a noisy party, but something deeper, something real.

Hours passed unnoticed until Tori glanced at her watch. "Wow, it's really late," she said, surprised.

"Time flies when you're enjoying yourself," Antonio said, a hint of reluctance in his voice. "Should I walk you back downstairs?"

"Yeah, I think that might be a good idea," Tori agreed, standing up.

SIR JONTONIO

Antonio led her back down the hallway and they descended the staircase. The party was still in full swing, but it felt like a different world now.

"Thanks for the drink and the great conversation," Tori said.

"Anytime," Antonio replied. "I really enjoyed tonight."

"Me too," Tori said, giving him a warm smile before blending back into the lively crowd. Antonio watched her go, already looking forward to their next meeting.

Chapter 5

Sisterhood and Secrets

Andrea sat in the living room, basking in the gentle afternoon light streaming through the curtains. A broad smile stretched across her face as she ended the phone call. She had been apprehensive about Antonio not showing up the previous night, but their conversation had cleared the air. He had apologized and agreed to go to church with her, which was a huge relief.

On the couch, her two sisters, Erica and Dondria, lounged casually, half-watching TV but more interested in eavesdropping on Andrea's conversation. Erica, the eldest, had a knack for giving unsolicited advice, and Dondria, the youngest, was just as ready to chime in.

"Girl, you know he is playing you, right?" Erica said, not looking up from the TV.

"I would have been pissed if he stood me up," Dondria added, her tone resonating with a mix of seriousness and sass.

"You think I wasn't?" Andrea shot back, a hint of frustration in her voice.

"I know you were, but you forgave him too fast," Dondria said, her eyes narrowing slightly.

"Drea, you not going to sit there and act like you didn't hear me talking to you," Erica said, her tone edging into irritation.

"Erica, shut up and stop being so bitter. Leave that girl alone," Dondria interjected.

"Don't tell me to shut up. Y'all know I'm right. Who are you calling bitter? I wasn't so bitter when you needed a ride because your lil' boo couldn't pick you up from work now, was I?" Erica countered, her voice rising.

"Ladies! Ladies! Calm down. Dondria, girl, you know I love you, and thank you, but I got Erica," Andrea said, trying to inject some calm into the escalating tension.

"You got me?" Erica asked, a curious look crossing her face.

"Yeah, I got you. I love you, really, I do—but lately, you've been acting really salty, and I know something is up. So, spill the tea," Andrea said, her tone soft but firm.

"Salty? Who are you calling salty, Drea?" Erica bristled.

Andrea's cellphone buzzed, stealing everyone's attention. Dondria, ever the opportunist, grabbed it and read the incoming text. "Bae, I'm sorry for standing you up last night," she read aloud.

"You!" Dondria exclaimed, looking at her sisters.

"Sis, I love you but honestly, since you and Jamal broke up, you have really been on one," Andrea said, eyeing Erica cautiously.

"Jamal? Ain't nobody worried about him. He does not dictate anything over here," Erica said, her voice faltering slightly.

"Girl, see, that's what we're talking about. You let that lil' boy steal your joy, and the worst part is, you can't admit that you're hurting. Sis, I look up to you," Dondria said, reaching out to touch Erica's hand.

"I know I deserve better, but it's something about him I can't shake. I can't lie; I miss how close we used to be, but he makes me feel like I have to compete with Andrea," Erica admitted, a tear catching at the edge of her eye.

"Compete with me, how? You know we are sisters, and we don't compete over anything. There is no competition," Andrea said, her voice filled with genuine concern.

"Easy for you to say. You always get what you want, and you are always the center of attention," Erica said, her voice breaking a little.

FOOL'S GOLD

"I'm sorry that you feel that way. To be honest, I always looked up to you and wanted to be like you. You're the reason why I sing and grind so hard," Andrea said, pulling Erica and Dondria into a hug. The warmth of the hug started to dissolve the tension that had been building up, but the moment was interrupted by a ringing phone.

Erica glanced at it, her heart skipping a beat when she saw Jamal's name light up the screen. "Hey sweetie. How have you been?" Jamal's voice sounded gentle but insistent.

"What do you want, Jamal?" Erica's voice was curt, her body tensing.

"What's up with the attitude?" Jamal asked, confusion detectable in his tone.

"Nothing," Erica said, softer, but still guarded.

"Best friend, what's wrong?" Jamal probed.

"I said nothing. Why did you call me? I haven't talked to you in a week," Erica said, her voice softening even as her frustration increased.

"Because I miss you. I haven't talked to you in a week because I lost my phone, and I just got this new one," Jamal said.

"Really? Do you think I was born last night? Bye, Jamal. You really think I'm stupid to believe a half-thought-out lie?" Erica said, ready to hang up.

"It's the truth. I really did lose my phone and had to wait till I got paid to get a new one," Jamal insisted.

"Yeah, yeah, whatever," Erica said, rolling her eyes.

"I had to call you because I realize how special you are to me and after last night, I didn't want to wait another day to tell you how I feel," Jamal continued.

"What do you mean after what happened last night?" Erica asked, curiosity piqued.

"This nigga Jacob almost got us shot last night," Jamal said.

"Wait a minute, did you say that Jacob almost got you shot?" Erica said, now fully engaged in the conversation.

"Yes, Jacob was really on one. Like this nigga was drinking and smoking. He spilled his drink on this chick's shirt and started fussing with her and then her guy got involved," Jamal explained.

"So, Jacob smokes and drinks now? That boy ain't built like that. What happened when the other guy stepped in?" Erica asked.

"Jacob flashed a gun, and I saw things getting really bad really quick," Jamal said, his voice shaking a little.

"When did he get a gun?" Erica's voice wavered.

"I don't know. But the guy is from the View, and he don't play. Like homie is about that life," Jamal said.

"I can't believe it. I'm glad you're okay, boo. Well, look, I have to go. I will call you later," Erica said, her voice now filled with concern and frustration in equal measures.

"Okay, how about I come get you after the wedding?" Jamal suggested.

"What wedding? Who's getting married?" Erica asked, perplexed.

"This guy that goes to my uncle's church," Jamal said.

"Oh, okay. Well, tell Pastor Anderson I said hello," Erica said softly, her guard dropping a bit.

"Okay, bae. I'll see you later," Jamal said, the warmth returning to his voice.

"Be safe. Oh, I miss you too, big head," Erica said, ending the call with a bittersweet smile.

As Erica put her phone down, she saw her sisters looking at her with expressions that mixed relief and concern. The three of them, enveloped in the warmth and complexity of their bond, shared a moment of silence before returning to the chaotic, beautiful reality of their lives.

Chapter 6

Morning After and Wedding Bells

Tori lay in her bed, the morning light filtering softly through the curtains. She was lost in her thoughts about Antonio, replaying the events of the previous night. She started talking to herself out loud, chuckling softly. "Last night was something different. I can't believe he did that," she murmured. A vivid flashback of the party emerged in her mind's eye. Laughing, she said, "And he really had me dancing." She rolled over, playing with her hair, feeling the warmth of those memories. "I'm glad I went to that party last night," she thought aloud. "I really enjoyed myself."

As if on cue, her friend Kim knocked and simultaneously pushed the door open. "Girl, Tori, get up. I know you ain't sleep," Kim announced.

"Hey, Kim," Tori responded, her voice dripping with sarcasm. "What's the point of having a door if people just gonna walk in? What if I had a lil dip in here?" she said, rolling her eyes dramatically.

"I walk in because I know you're not doing anything," Kim replied. Laughing, she added, "Lil dip? Girl, please. We know you ain't dipping nothing."

"Who ain't dipping? Now you know I dip my wings in that buffalo sauce," Tori shot back, prompting both of them to burst into laughter.

"Speaking of dipping, what happened to you last night? I seen you dancing. And we know you don't be dancing like that in a club," Kim said, her curiosity piqued.

SIR JONTONIO

"Girl, I didn't even know him like that. But he knew me. Like, this man knew what type of drink I drank," Tori recalled, her voice tinged with excitement.

"So? What that mean? Everybody knows you like clear," Kim stated matter-of-factly.

"I don't like clear. I drink clear 'cause y'all can't handle the brown," Tori retorted.

"Whatever. So, what happened last night?" Kim pressed.

"I walked up to him and asked him; did I know him?" Tori continued.

"So, you knew him?" Kim's eyebrows raised in curiosity.

"No, not really. I've seen him a few times at parties on campus," Tori admitted.

"Oh, okay. So, you been boo'ed up? Can't believe you've been hiding him," Kim teased.

Just then, Tori's phone buzzed with a text from Antonio. The message read, "Hey, how are you doing today?"

"See, this is him now," Tori said, showing Kim the text. She quickly replied, "Hey, you. I'm doing good. How are you doing today?"

A swift reply came back: "LOL, I'm doing good, thanks for asking."

"Girl, he just started laughing. I don't see nothing funny," Tori said, frowning.

"Why is he laughing? What did you say?" Kim asked, her eyes narrowing.

"I said, 'Hey, you. How are you doing today?'" Tori repeated.

"Did you really say 'hey, you'? Who says that? I would have laughed too," Kim said, still giggling.

"I don't know why. What else was I supposed to say?" Tori asked, genuinely puzzled.

"Hey boo. Hey bae. Hey sweetheart or something. Girl, my grandmother and her friends be saying 'hey you' when they be trying to flirt with them young boys at the store," Kim said, snickering.

FOOL'S GOLD

"Well, I didn't know what to say. So, I said what I said how I said it," Tori defended herself.

Tori sent another text to Antonio, "What's so funny?"

He texted back, "You are funny."

"How am I funny?" Tori typed, her fingers moving swiftly over the screen.

"Hey, you. LOL. Who says that?" Antonio replied.

"I say it. Problem?" Tori shot back.

"Nah, love, you got it. Just thought it was cute," Antonio texted.

"Cute, huh? I know you gonna stop playing with me," Tori typed, smiling.

"Yeah, I thought it was cute. But I was texting to say hey. Plus, I wanted to see what you were doing," Antonio replied.

"I ain't doing nothing but talking to my friend Kim," Tori texted back.

"Hey, Kim. But go ahead and finish doing what you were doing. I didn't want anything," Antonio responded.

"Oh okay. So, what are you doing today?" Tori asked.

"Headed to my boy Zeke's wedding," Antonio mentioned casually.

"Oh wow, I'll be there too," Tori exclaimed aloud, looking at Kim.

"You coming through?" Antonio asked.

"Yes, I'm coming. Zeke is Kim's cousin. She came over to get ready," Tori explained.

"Oh okay. I think I know who you're talking about. But I'll see you there," Antonio said.

"Ok. See ya there," Tori replied, placing her phone on the bed with a satisfied smile.

Kim arched an eyebrow at Tori. "You are so disrespectful."

"How am I disrespectful?" Tori asked, feigning innocence.

"You ignored me and started texting. So, who was it?" Kim pried.

"It was Tonio, the guy from last night," Tori clarified.

SIR JONTONIO

"Last night, huh? So, what happened? I saw you dancing, drinking, and even had a lil nightcap," Kim said, her tone filled with amusement.

"Nothing happened. Yeah, we danced, and yeah, we drank Henny but honestly, when we went upstairs, things were very different and plus, I needed that," Tori said, starting to play with her hair again.

"You are nasty," Kim teased, laughing. "Was it good?"

"Girl, nothing happened. Last night really did something to me. I can't lie," Tori said, her tone softening.

"Well, since you are talking in circles, get up, take a shower, and get dressed so we can go," Kim commanded.

"Why are you in a rush?" Tori asked, getting out of bed.

"I'm trying to see Brandon," Kim admitted, a sly smile spreading across her face.

"Brandon? Who is Brandon?" Tori asked, her curiosity piqued.

"The guy who was lit the whole night," Kim explained, her eyes sparkling with excitement.

Laughing, Tori said, "That fool was lit and going hard, alright."

"Girl, who are you telling?" Kim replied, her grin widening. "I just made it home. But he said he wanted to meet up at my cousin's wedding."

"Alright, give me a minute," Tori said, heading to the shower.

Kim walked out of the room; the excitement of the day ahead lingering in the air. A few moments later, they left the house, ready for Zeke's wedding and all the adventures the day would bring.

Chapter 7

Calls and Commitments

Andrea was in her bedroom, balancing her phone between her ear and shoulder while putting on mascara. She was getting ready to leave, but first, she had to finish her conversation with Jacob. The screen flickered as Antonio's name beeped in, indicating an incoming call. She decided to stick with Jacob for the moment.

"Look who finally decided to call," Andrea said, her tone both teasing and slightly irritated.

"Don't do that. My flight got delayed, and I got in late last night," Jacob replied defensively.

"You couldn't call or text me to let me know what was going on?" Andrea asked, her voice softening with genuine concern.

"Like I said, it was late, and I thought you were asleep. I didn't want to disturb you. You know Daddy will make it up to you. You can have whatever you like, and we'll do whatever you want," Jacob said, warming up his voice to appease her.

"So what time are you coming? You know I don't have all day," Andrea said, glancing at her reflection in the mirror.

"I'm on my way now," Jacob replied quickly.

"Good, I'm hungry and I need a new dress to go with my new purse," Andrea stated.

SIR JONTONIO

"What new purse?" Jacob queried, feigning ignorance. Andrea's thoughts drifted to Antonio, who had gifted her the latest accessory. Smiling to herself, she replied, "Now you know I know who the plug is."

"Plug? Girl, the only plug you know is Daddy," Jacob said, laughing. "Nah, I'm playing. We can go eat first and then get you a dress."

"Ok, call me when you're outside. Bye," Andrea instructed.

As soon as she hung up with Jacob, Andrea called Antonio back. "Tonioooooooo. Antonio," she sang into the phone.

"Yeah bae. What's up?" Antonio's voice came through, mingled with the sound of laughter from another guy. "You are wild, bro," he said to someone in the background.

"Tonio, what are you doing?" Andrea asked.

"On my way to the wedding with my bro Brandon," Antonio replied.

"Tell Brandon I said hey. How long you think you're going to be at the wedding?" Andrea asked, her eyes flicking to the clock.

"I'm not telling that nigga nothing," Antonio said, laughing. "Nah, I'm playing. Drea said Hey, bro," he relayed to Brandon. "But I don't know how long we will be at the wedding. Why, what's up?" Antonio asked, turning his attention back to Andrea.

"Just asking 'cause I miss you and really want to see you," Andrea said softly.

"I miss you too. We can link after the reception," Antonio suggested.

"What time will that be over? You know I have church in the morning," Andrea said, her voice tinged with impatience.

"So, you don't wanna link up?" Antonio questioned.

"Yes, I want to chill but I'm not trying to be out all late," Andrea replied.

Just then, she heard a honk outside. She peered out the window to see Jacob's car.

"Who is that?" Antonio asked, suspicion creeping into his voice.

"That's my people. I'm about to go shopping and get something to eat," Andrea said casually.

FOOL'S GOLD

"Where you going to get something to eat from?" Antonio asked, curiosity piqued.

"I don't know yet. I haven't made up my mind. Why?" Andrea responded.

"Save me some," Antonio said, his tone playful.

"You know I got you. And I'm going to get something I know you will like," Andrea assured him.

"Oh yeah? We gonna see. Well, hit me up later," Antonio said.

"Ok baby. Love you. Talk to you later," Andrea said.

"Love you too," Antonio replied before hanging up.

Andrea grabbed her purse and headed outside to Jacob's car. She slid into the passenger seat, closing the door behind her.

"Dang, you took too long," Andrea teased as Jacob drove away.

"It wasn't that long. What's up? Why are you bugging?" Jacob asked, glancing at her.

"Because I missed you. Glad we're finally spending time," Andrea said, smiling at him.

"I missed you too. So, have you made your mind up yet?" Jacob asked.

"Made my mind up about what?" Andrea asked, looking puzzled.

"About what you want to eat," Jacob clarified.

"I want some shrimp pasta with some baked fish," Andrea declared, her eyes lighting up at the thought.

"Ok. So do you want to go to a restaurant, or do you want me to cook?" Jacob offered.

"I would rather you cook. So, we could just shop and chill," Andrea said, leaning back in her seat.

"Ok. So, what type of dress you trying to get?" Jacob asked.

"I want a dress to match this cute purse," Andrea said, showing off the stylish handbag.

"That's a nice purse. Who got you that?" Jacob asked, his eyes narrowing slightly.

SIR JONTONIO

"My people got it for me. I love it though. I was thinking about getting something for Friday," Andrea said.

"Friday? What's going on Friday?" Jacob asked.

"Just meeting up with a friend and hanging out. Well, probably catch a movie or something," Andrea explained.

"Oh, okay. Well, I would have loved to meet them, but I'm going out of town," Jacob said.

"Out of town? How long are you going to be gone?" Andrea asked, surprise evident in her voice.

"About a week and a half," Jacob replied.

"Damn, that's a long time. When do you leave?" Andrea asked, her tone shifting to concern.

"Tomorrow night," Jacob said.

"How am I going to spend time with you if you're always gone?" Andrea asked, her voice tinged with frustration.

"I know it sucks, but I'll be back. You know I think about you when I'm always gone," Jacob tried to reassure her.

"Yeah, yeah, tell me anything," Andrea said, rolling her eyes.

"I'm serious. Look, let's enjoy the time we do have, okay?" Jacob said, turning to her briefly.

"Ok, bae," Andrea said, smiling.

Jacob turned up the radio as they drove away, both trying to make the most of the day ahead.

Chapter 8

Bridging Paths and New Beginnings

Pastor Anderson made his way down the narrow corridor, the scent of fresh flowers mingling with the anticipation in the air. Bridesmaids and groomsmen hustled back and forth, laughter and last-minute instructions mingling with the sounds of classical music being rehearsed by the string quartet in the main hall. He approached a door, the wooden surface adorned with a simple sign that read, "Groom's Room." Pastor Anderson knocked gently.

"Hello, Zeke, are you busy? May I come in?" Pastor Anderson asked.

Inside, Zeke was standing before a full-length mirror, adjusting his bow tie. His hands were slightly trembling, a mix of excitement and nerves. He turned and smiled upon hearing the familiar voice. "Nah, I'm not busy, and you may enter."

The door creaked open, and Pastor Anderson stepped inside, his presence immediately bringing a sense of calm and wisdom. His warm, steady gaze took in the room, noting the heirloom watch Zeke's grandfather had worn on his wedding day now sitting on a nearby table.

"So, today is the day. Are you ready?" Pastor Anderson asked with a kind smile.

Laughing, Zeke replied, "I better be because if I wasn't ready, it's too late now. We're here."

"Yeah, it would be too late," Pastor Anderson chuckled, his eyes twinkling. "How are you feeling? What's going on through your mind?"

"Honestly, I'm nervous because this is really a life-changing moment," Zeke confessed, his voice tinged with sincerity. "I really want to be the best man I can be and the best husband for Miranda."

"Well, son, that's understandable and expected. You're supposed to be feeling those exact feelings. Own this moment and be the best husband you can be by putting and keeping God first so He can mold you into the best man you need to be." He placed a reassuring hand on Zeke's shoulder, feeling the tension ease slightly under his touch.

"Thanks, Pastor Anderson. You always seem to know what to say and when to say it. I wish you could speak some sense into my best man," Zeke said with a laugh.

"No problem, that's why I'm here, Zeke. It's my job to share encouraging words with God's people. And tell me more about your friend," Pastor Anderson said, his curiosity piqued.

"His name is Antonio," Zeke began. "He's really a cool guy, honestly. He has so much knowledge and so much influence that could be used to build up the Kingdom."

"Well, does he go to church?" Pastor Anderson inquired, raising an eyebrow.

Laughing, Zeke replied, "Does he go to church? Shoot, I was surprised when he said he was coming here today."

"Zeke, it can't be that bad, can it?" Pastor Anderson asked, his curiosity deepening.

"Honestly, I don't know the details of why he stopped going, but he does know about God and The Word of God," Zeke admitted, his eyes troubled. "He just chooses not to attend church."

Pastor Anderson's expression softened. "Well, it's good he knows who God is and has knowledge of God's Word. Proverbs 22:6 says, 'Train up a child in the way he should go: and when he is old, he will not depart from it.'"

"Yeah, he does, but I feel like there is so much he has to offer, and he doesn't even want to be part of any type of organization that involves church," Zeke explained, frustration edging his voice. "Like, you should see how he walks into parties and takes command of the whole place—the people really love this guy."

Outside the room, Antonio and Brandon approached, laughter in their voices as they walked down the hall.

"Yo, you think Zeke is in there crying?" Brandon joked.

Laughing, Antonio replied, "Crying? Why would he be crying?"

"Now you know bro is softer than Cottonelle," Brandon said.

"Now you know Zeke ain't soft. I'm still shocked that he's really getting married," Antonio said.

"I know. I'm just joking. For real though, Miranda has made that dude so emotional and so sensitive," Brandon added.

"I won't say emotional and sensitive. He just found someone that he knows he can settle down with and build a family with. Honestly, I like Miranda—not only did she get Zeke to change his life, but she also got him to go to church," Antonio said.

"Blah blah blah, what are you saying, Tonio? You sound like you're ready to preach a sermon," Brandon teased.

"No, I ain't tryna preach. I'm just saying it would be nice to meet someone that would make life better. After all, the good book says that it is not good for man to be alone," Antonio said.

They reached the door, and Antonio knocked, laughing. "Zekey Weeky. Stop playing with yo lil' wee wee."

Laughing, Brandon added, "Yeah, you know your momma told you that it's inappropriate in public and that you can go blind. As a matter of fact, Mrs. Lee is right down the hall. Mrs. Lee, guess what Zeke is..."

Zeke interrupted, "Brandon, chill, and Antonio, you're not funny. Come in and stop playing in the hallway like some kids."

"Kids? You're the one that sounds like a kid talking about stop playing in the hallway, like you gonna get in trouble. Nigga, we grown—who gonna tell on us?" Brandon retorted.

SIR JONTONIO

"Well, it is inappropriate to play in the house of the Lord," Pastor Anderson said, stepping into their banter.

"It's also inappropriate to be religious and teach people things based off of how your flesh is feeling," Antonio responded.

"Hello, Antonio. How are you doing?" Pastor Anderson asked, offering his hand.

"What's up? I'm good," Antonio said, brushing Pastor off before turning to Zeke. "So, Zeke, how are you feeling, big dawg?"

"Honestly, I was nervous but now that you and Brandon are here, I'm good. Aye, why y'all so late anyways?" Zeke asked.

"'Cause Mr. Fabio Hefner wanna take a million years to get dressed like he had to pick an outfit out," Brandon teased.

Laughing, Zeke asked, "I can see that, but where does the Hefner come from?"

"You boy, you were macking hard last night and didn't come home 'til this morning," Brandon said.

"Oh, yeah? I thought I seen you go upstairs with the shawty with the coke bottle shape. Did you satisfy your..." Zeke began before Antonio interjected, catching Pastor Anderson's eye.

"Nah, I'm not Hefner. And it was nothing last night," Antonio said with finality.

"Well, I have to go. I will see you guys in a few," Pastor Anderson said, sensing it was time to give the men a moment alone.

"Ok, Pastor. See you in a few. So, what happened? I seen you talking, dancing, and drinking then you just disappeared," Zeke said.

Laughing, Brandon added, "Like Houdini and oh girl was his ASS-istant."

"Honestly, nothing, bro. Look, are we going to sit here talking the whole time, or you gonna go become a changed man and marry your rib?" Antonio said, steering the conversation back to the wedding.

"Don't try to change the subject, Craig. You ain't gotta lie. But I am ready to see the guy walk down this aisle," Brandon said.

"Well, let's go then," Zeke said, straightening his jacket. As they walked toward the sanctuary, Tori and Kim walked through the door, momentarily halting Antonio in his tracks.

"Hey, you. You clean up nice and look very handsome," Tori said, smiling.

"Hey, beautiful. You look amazing and you're breathtaking," Antonio replied, his eyes locking onto hers. The group continued to the sanctuary, each step filled with anticipation and the gravity of the moment. Today wasn't just about vows and rings; it was about bridging paths, finding new directions, and celebrating the bonds that held them all together.

Chapter 9
Crew Love and Pre-Wedding Banter

Antonio and Tori walked up to each other just before the wedding began, the atmosphere electric with excitement and anticipation. Brandon introduced himself with a friendly smile, and Zeke quickly revealed that Kim was his cousin.

"Thank you, and you look very handsome. You are wearing that suit very well, sir," Tori said, her eyes sparkling.

"Thank you, ma'am," Antonio replied, nodding.

"Excuse me, girl, who is this?" Kim asked, her curiosity piqued.

"What's up, love? My name is Antonio," he said, extending a hand.

"Heyyyyy. My name is Kim. Tori, girl, you didn't tell me he was this good-looking, and his smile is to die for," Kim said, turning slightly to Tori.

Tori blushed and said, "Girl, stop, you are embarrassing me."

"What did you just say about my brother?" Brandon asked, stepping closer with a wide grin.

"Hey boo, this is your brother?" Kim asked, raising an eyebrow.

"Yeah, this is my brother. Tonio, this is the shawty from last night I was telling you about," Brandon said.

"Oh, okay. I thought she looked familiar. But I feel like I know you from somewhere, though," Antonio said, knitting his brows together.

"Nah, you don't know me. If you did, we wouldn't be standing here right now," Kim replied, smirking.

"Girl, you are nasty. Sit yo hot self down somewhere," Tori said, rolling her eyes.

"Hot? Girl, please, I'm just saying," Kim said, shrugging.

Zeke looked over at Kim and grinned. "Hey, lil' cousin."

"Hey, big cuz. You are looking sharp. Are you sure you want to do this? 'Because you know I will shut this whole thing down," Kim said with a wicked smile.

Laughing, Zeke replied, "Yeah, I am sure. And I know you will shut it down. You just like yo momma."

Antonio turned to Kim, "See, I told you I knew you from somewhere. Last year at your family reunion, you were turnt up at the after-party."

"Yeah, that's right. I remember now. How have you been?" Kim asked, her expression softening.

"I've been good. How about yourself? How do y'all know each other, and why didn't you bring her with you last year?" Antonio questioned.

"I was there. You were too busy doing you," Tori said, smirking sarcastically.

"Hey, I'm Brandon. My brother is so rude," Brandon interjected.

"Hello, I'm Tori. You look very nice," Tori said, smiling.

"Thank you," Brandon replied.

"Why didn't you text me when you made it up here?" Kim asked, turning to Brandon.

"To be honest, when we got here, we started talking to this guy and Tonio went in on the Pastor," Brandon said with a laugh. "That boy ain't got no type of home training."

"Shut up, Brandon. Don't get him started again," Zeke chimed in.

Tori turned to Antonio, "So, you just snapping on everybody, huh? Let me not get on your bad side."

"Nah, it's not like that. You are good, my love. You could never get on my bad side as long as you always be honest," Antonio said, his voice gentle.

"I got you," Tori replied, her smile widening.

"So, which one of y'all is my cousin's best man?" Kim asked, looking between Antonio and Brandon.

"Both of us. I don't know why Tonio's one, I knew Zeke longer," Brandon said.

"Because I'm the one that introduced him to his wife," Antonio countered.

"Introduced? Boy, you call that an introduction. You were supposed to go on a date with her and you bailed out and sent Zeke instead," Brandon said.

Laughing, Antonio said, "Yeah, if it wasn't for me, they wouldn't have met. And the only reason why I bailed was because you told me to come be your wingman at this party you invited to. And the worst part is you didn't get no play that night."

"I wasn't trying to holla at nobody there. That party was whack," Brandon said, shrugging.

"Whack? Really? I had a phenomenal night that night," Antonio said, smiling broadly.

"I bet you did, Mr. Steal yo girl," Brandon said with a chuckle.

"Who girl did I steal? I can't help that I was chosen," Antonio said, laughing.

"Okay, super fly," Brandon said, just as Zeke cut in, "Y'all ready? We can continue this walk down Brandon's no-game-having life later."

"Awww Brandon, you don't have game, baby?" Tori teased, stifling a laugh.

"Don't ask me that. I don't know why you listening to these fools," Brandon said, shaking his head.

Laughing, Kim said, "Oh, someone salty, huh?"

Brandon turned to Kim, "Salty? What time you make it home this morning?"

"So, you know I was playing, boo. Your game is on point. Had to have some type of game to get all of this," Kim said with a wink.

"What? Brandon, you got with my cousin?" Zeke asked, his eyes wide with surprise.

Tori tried to divert the attention away from Brandon and Kim. "Zeke, you look amazing, and your wife is a lucky gal. Tonio, I will see you later. Oh, and thanks for last night. Really needed that. Come on, Kim, let's go get our seats. Bye, y'all."

"Thank you, beautiful. Brandon don't think I will forget about this talk we will have about my cousin," Zeke said, giving Brandon a pointed look.

"Yeah, yeah, yeah, see y'all," Brandon said and turned to tease Antonio. "Tonio, I will see you later. Nothing happened. Yeah, right. Stevie Wonder must have 20/20 vision now 'cause you lying, B."

Laughing, Antonio said, "Chill, bro, she can still hear you. And NOTHING HAPPENED!!"

"I don't know...these vibes I'm sensing ain't adding up to what you saying," Zeke said, starting to laugh. "Can't believe I'm saying this, but I think I agree with Brandon."

"Hell must have frozen over 'cause y'all don't never agree. Man let's get you to the altar before your soon-to-be wife kill all three of us," Antonio said, urging them to move.

"If she does, you shouldn't trip, Tonio," Brandon said with a grin.

"Why you say that?" Antonio asked, curious.

"'Cause all dogs go to Heaven," Brandon said, laughing.

They all shared a hearty laugh as they walked into the church to get into position. The camaraderie was palpable, a testament to their deep bonds and shared histories. Each step towards the altar was filled with a blend of joy, anticipation, and light-hearted banter, marking the beginning of a memorable day.

Chapter 10

Heartfelt Promises

Jacob stood at the stove; the kitchen filled with the savory aromas of a meal in progress. The clinking of pots and the sizzling of ingredients provided a comforting backdrop to the conversation he was having with Andrea. She sat at the kitchen island, a playful smile on her lips as she watched him work.

"I hope you enjoy this meal that I'm cooking for you," Jacob said, glancing over his shoulder with a smile.

Laughing, Andrea replied, "Now you know I will 'cause I'm a big girl at heart."

Jacob chuckled, shaking his head. "Yeah, I know. You just ate all my grapes. How do you know I didn't want any?"

"You couldn't tell? You were the one trying to be all romantic by feeding me grapes," Andrea teased back.

"Girl, I only fed you three," Jacob said, grinning.

"Whatever, boy. But I really love the dress you bought me. Thank you, babe," Andrea said, her voice softening as she admired the elegant dress draped over the back of a chair.

"I knew you would. Daddy knows what his baby girl likes," Jacob said, pride evident in his tone.

"Daddy? Huh?" Andrea asked, arching an eyebrow.

"Yup. That's what you were saying earlier. 'Oh, Daddy. Big Daddy. Big Daddy, please. Give it to me. Please, don't stop,'" Jacob mimicked, bursting into laughter as he recalled their earlier intimacy.

"Shut up. You are not funny. You play too much," Andrea said, trying to suppress a giggle. "You never answered my question from earlier."

"What question?" Jacob asked innocently.

"Jacob, seriously?" Andrea said, giving him a pointed look.

"Alright, alright, I'm just playing. Babe, as long as we keep God in the midst, we will last," Jacob said, his tone turning serious.

"How do you know? I'm not trying to get hurt," Andrea said softly, her eyes reflecting her vulnerability.

Jacob turned off the stove and walked over to her, taking her hands in his. He gazed deeply into her eyes, his expression earnest. "Baby, you are my world, my rib, my peace, and I promise I'll make a fighting effort to show you that I'm grateful to have you in my life."

Tears welled up in Andrea's eyes, but she managed to smile. "You don't mean that. Jacob, I don't want to get hurt."

"Baby, we are in this until the wheels fall off. I just want you to be secure in us. I told your father I was going to make you my wife, and I mean that," Jacob said, his voice firm with conviction. He leaned in and kissed her, sealing his promise with a gesture that spoke volumes.

Andrea felt her fears melting away, replaced by a warmth that spread through her chest. "Okay," she whispered. "I trust you."

Jacob smiled, kissed her forehead, and returned to the stove to finish cooking. The kitchen was silent for a moment, with only the sounds of cooking filling the air. Andrea watched him, feeling a newfound sense of security.

As Jacob stirred the pot, he began to talk again. "You know, I've been thinking a lot about our future. About what it looks like if we both make sacrifices to be together."

"What kind of sacrifices?" Andrea asked, intrigued.

FOOL'S GOLD

"Well, maybe I don't travel as much. Maybe I find work that keeps me closer to home. And maybe you can come with me on some of the trips that are unavoidable. It's about compromise, babe," Jacob explained.

Andrea nodded thoughtfully. "I like the sound of that. I want to be a part of your life completely, not just in the moments you're home."

Jacob smiled, his heart swelling with love and pride. "And I want you with me, always. We'll figure it out. Together."

Andrea's phone buzzed on the counter, breaking the intimate moment. She glanced at the screen and saw a message from her best friend, Tori: *Can't wait to hear about dinner with Jacob! Call me later.* Andrea quickly typed a response: *I will. It's going great.*

"Who's that?" Jacob asked, finishing up the dishes.

"Tori. She's dying to know how our dinner goes," Andrea said with a laugh.

"Ah, the infamous Tori. Tell her I'm treating you right, or she'll come after me," Jacob said, grinning.

"She might just do that," Andrea joked. "I'm lucky to have her in my corner."

"You're lucky to have a lot of people in your corner. I'm one of them," Jacob said, plating the food and setting it on the island in front of Andrea. He leaned down to kiss her cheek gently. "I love you, Andrea."

"I love you too, Jacob," Andrea replied, her heart full as they began to eat the meal, he had lovingly prepared.

As they savored the meal, their conversation continued, weaving through dreams for their future, shared laughs, and plans to navigate the complexity of their lives together. Each moment, each word, brought them closer, bonding their hearts and solidifying their commitment to one another.

The night faded into a comfortable silence, both wrapped in the warmth of their love and the promise of what was to come. This was not just another meal; it was a step towards a future filled with trust, love, and unwavering faith. For Andrea, this moment was a reassurance that no matter the distance or the challenges ahead, Jacob was truly committed to being her partner in every sense. And for Jacob, it was a reminder of why he was willing to fight for this relationship, willing to make sacrifices and changes, because Andrea was worth it all.

Chapter 11

The Vows of Love and Faith

The air was filled with anticipation as the wedding ceremony of Zeke and Miranda was about to begin. Guests settled into their seats, and a gentle murmur filled the sanctuary. Off to the side, Antonio and Brandon joined the rest of the groomsmen, their excitement mirrored by the glowing bridesmaids. Meanwhile, Andrea sat at Jacob's house, texting Tori. The aroma of Jacob's cooking filled the room.

Tori: I was gonna come see you, but your sis said that you were with Jacob. Who is Jacob?

Andrea: Oh, he's just a friend. Why? Is everything okay? Is Tonio there?

Tori: Yes, but your boyfriend almost got shot last night.

Andrea: Shot? What happened?

Tori: This drunk fool decided to bump into me and spill all his drink on me. And all I'm saying is things got real heated real fast, but I guess Tonio got some type of clout.

Andrea: Oh, so my baby a hood guy? I got me a roughneck. I like that.

Tori: Well, I'll text you later. The wedding is about to start.

Andrea: Ok. Are you meeting with Antonio afterwards?

Tori: I don't know; I'm kinda tired from last night. Tonio didn't bring me home 'til 7 or 8 something this morning.

Andrea: Wait, what? Never mind that; you better stick to the plan. Bye.

Tori: Bye.

SIR JONTONIO

Andrea tucked her phone away just as the ceremony commenced. Pastor Anderson stood before the congregation, his demeanor both serene and noble.

"We are gathered here today to join these two lovely people together in Holy Matrimony. I have known Zeke and Miranda for some time now, and I am truly honored to be standing here to officiate this union of these two Holy Ghost-filled believers. The lovely couple decided that they wanted to write their own vows and share them with each other today. So, we are going to start with Miranda," Pastor Anderson announced.

Miranda took a deep breath, her eyes locking onto Zeke's. "Thank you, Pastor Anderson," Miranda began. "Zeke, you are my everything. I am so glad that I am standing here today before God, family, and friends to say I do. The Bible says that I am your rib, and I am so thankful to be made from someone who is so loving and kind. Before I met you, I was the simple church girl that didn't pay no guy any attention because I knew that I wasn't ready to love anyone but God. Every day I prayed that God would protect my husband wherever he was and really teach me how to be the wife, lover, supporter, and friend that he will need. The first time I saw you, I thought, 'Oh, he's kinda cute,' but you were rough around the edges," Miranda said, eliciting a chuckle from the audience. "Then when I saw you accept God and begin to follow Christ, I knew that I would love no other man but you. The day you asked me on a date was the day I heard God say, 'The race is not given to the swift, but to those who endure to the end.' So, I am standing here to say, baby, I love you, and I am here to stay and support you throughout this journey called life. And I'm grateful that you asked me to be your wife."

"Hallelujah. Those words were truly from the heart, and I know that God led every word," Pastor Anderson said, a tear glistening in his eye. "It is truly amazing to see the love of God surrounding the two of you at this moment. Zeke, it's your turn to share your vows."

"Thank you, Pastor," Zeke started, his voice strong yet emotional. "Baby girl, I love you so much. For weeks I wondered what I was gonna say today for my vows, and I must have written on at least a thousand papers to make sure I said the correct things. But now I realize that no matter what I wrote, words from my heart could never be wrong.

"First, I gotta thank God for allowing me to be standing here with the opportunity to become your husband. Secondly, I wanna thank you for saving me and showing me that real love is obtainable. I was so lost and hurt before you came into my life. Baby, with God's grace, you healed a part of me that was so damaged. My heart. Before I came to church and fell in love with God, I had no purpose, and I treated every female I dealt with so wrong. I remember like it was yesterday when Pastor Anderson was preaching about Adam, and he said that God saw Adam working like he was created to do, and Adam was sad. He then said that God said it was not good for man to be alone, so he put Adam into a deep sleep and removed Adam's rib and created Eve. Baby, I was Adam, and although I had things in order in my life, I still felt something was missing. When you came up to me that day after the service, I knew you were flesh of my flesh and bone of my bones. Baby, you were my Eve. The Bible says that when a man finds a wife, he finds a good thing. Well, baby, you're my good thing, and I know I have obtained God's favor because everything that I go forth in it multiplies beautifully because of your support and encouragement even when I feel like giving up. So, on this day, I vow to love, honor, cherish, protect, provide, and cover you with prayers. I love you with all of my heart, and I can't wait to explore this journey called life with you as my best friend, lover, confidant, my rib, and my soul mate."

"Beautifully spoken by a true Man of God," Pastor Anderson said, his voice steady with emotion. "Zeke, I am so proud to see the Man of God you have grown to be. I know that this is only the beginning of the great things that God has planned for you." Turning to Miranda, Pastor Anderson continued, "Do you take this man to be your lawful husband, promise to love, honor, cherish, and respect through sickness and health until death do you part?"

"I do," Miranda said, her voice unwavering.

"Zeke, do you take this woman to be your lawful wife, promise to love, honor, cherish, and respect through sickness and health until death do you part?" Pastor Anderson asked.

"I do," Zeke replied, his gaze steady on Miranda.

"By the power vested in me by the Holy Spirit, I now pronounce you husband and wife. Zeke, you may kiss your bride," Pastor Anderson declared.

The congregation erupted in applause as Zeke and Miranda shared their first kiss as husband and wife. The joy in the room was palpable, each person presents a witness to the powerful love and commitment that Zeke and Miranda had just vowed to each other. As the couple walked down the aisle, arm in arm, they were met with smiles, cheers, and the occasional tear of joy.

Antonio watched them, feeling a sense of pride for his friend. He glanced at Tori, who was beaming, and felt a renewed sense of hope and possibility for their own relationship. For Zeke and Miranda, this was the start of a new, shared journey. And for everyone in attendance, it was a reminder of the power of love, faith, and the beautiful bonds that hold us all together.

Chapter 12

Embracing Vulnerability

Jacob and Andrea sat on the couch, the muted glow of the television casting soft shadows across their faces. They had just finished a delicious meal prepared by Jacob, but the atmosphere was thick with unspoken tension. Andrea stared at the screen, her thoughts a thousand miles away, while Jacob watched her, concerned.

"Did you enjoy your food, babe?" Jacob asked, trying to break the ice.

"Yup," Andrea replied curtly.

"Are you okay?" Jacob probed, sensing her unease.

"I'm fine," Andrea said, her eyes still fixed on the TV.

"Are you sure? You're giving me short answers and your whole demeanor shifted," Jacob pressed, his voice gently probing for the truth.

"I said I'm fine, Jacob," Andrea snapped.

Jacob took a deep breath, trying to keep his frustration in check. "Don't carry that tone with me. I know something is wrong, so just speak up. I'm not a mind reader, and if you're gonna sit with this funky attitude all night, I'll take you home. I didn't do anything to you for you to be snapping at me and giving short answers."

Andrea sighed, her shoulders slumping. "I know, babe, and I'm sorry for taking it out on you. It's just my friend texted me and told me something that upset me."

"Well, what did she say?" Jacob asked, shifting closer to her.

"She said that she got into it last night with some guy and things almost went left. Then on top of that, the guy she met at the party didn't bring her home until 7 or 8 this morning. I can't believe him," Andrea explained, her voice tinged with frustration.

"You can't believe him? What do you mean by that? She's grown; she could have left anytime she wanted to, right? Plus, if she met him there, that means she got to the party somehow. So, she could have left the way she got there," Jacob reasoned.

"Yeah, I can't believe him. Babe, he probably took advantage of my friend. Yes, she's grown, and yes, she could have left at any time she wanted. Her car is in the shop, so I dropped her off there to meet up with her roommate," Andrea said, her worry transforming into anger.

"If that's the case, why didn't you stay with her?" Jacob asked.

"Because I wanted to go home. Why would I go to a party with a bunch of guys when my man isn't here?" Andrea retorted.

"True. Babe, it must have been a crazy night for a lot of people then," Jacob said, trying to shift the conversation to a more neutral ground.

"Why do you say that boo?" Andrea asked, her curiosity piqued.

"Me and Jamal almost got into it with some guy last night, but we left so nothing major happened," Jacob revealed.

Laughing, Andrea said, "You and Jamal always getting into something and neither one of y'all can fight."

"Yeah, okay. If you think so. But seriously, don't shut down or snap on me like that again, okay?" Jacob advised; his voice gentle yet firm.

"Okay, daddy," Andrea responded, her tone lightening.

"So, what movie do you want to watch now?" Jacob asked, reaching for the remote.

"I don't want to watch a movie," Andrea said, scooting closer to him.

"Well, what do you wanna do?" Jacob asked, intrigued by her sudden change in mood.

"Let's go to the room. I want your lips to kiss all over my body," Andrea whispered in his ear, her breath sending shivers down his spine.

"Girl, stop playing," Jacob said, trying to keep his composure.

"I'm serious," Andrea said, standing up. She took his hand and led him towards the bedroom, her intentions clear.

Jacob followed her, his heartbeat quickening. As they stepped into the bedroom, Andrea closed the door behind them, shutting out the world. She turned to face him, her eyes filled with a mix of desire and determination.

"Come here," she whispered, pulling him towards the bed.

Jacob didn't need any more encouragement. He wrapped his arms around her, his lips finding hers in a passionate kiss. They tumbled onto the bed, their hands exploring each other with a fervor that spoke of weeks of pent-up longing and love.

Andrea felt her worries fade away with each kiss, each touch. She focused on Jacob, on the love they shared, allowing herself to be lost in the moment, forgetting about the texts and the troubles for a while.

Jacob, too, found solace in Andrea's embrace. He was determined to be the anchor she needed, to chase away her fears and frustrations. As they lay entwined, the bond between them grew stronger, fortified by their love and commitment to one another.

For the rest of the night, the couple found comfort and passion in each other's arms, a much-needed respite from the pressures and uncertainties of life. They talked, laughed, and loved, their hearts beating in unison. As dawn approached, they fell asleep in each other's arms, content and at peace. For that moment, nothing else mattered but the love they shared and the promise of a future together. And as they drifted off to sleep, the world outside seemed a little brighter, their worries a little lighter, and their love a lot stronger.

Chapter 13

My Sister's Keeper

Andrea lifted her gaze from her phone screen, memories from her past flooding her thoughts. She was planning to spend the weekend with Jacob, but her mind kept wandering back to when she and Tori first met and their adventures over the years. A gentle smile spread across her face thinking about how much had changed and how much had stayed the same.

The scent of freshly brewed coffee enveloped the cozy atmosphere of Starbucks as Andrea sat at a corner table, stirring her Frappuccino. The bell above the door chimed, and she looked up, recognizing the familiar face immediately.

"Tori," Andrea called out, her voice tinged with excitement.

Tori turned, her eyes brightening at the sight of her old friend. "Andrea, is that you? Hey, girl! How have you been?" she said as she walked over and gave Andrea a warm hug.

"I've been good. How have you been?" Andrea asked, returning the hug with equal enthusiasm.

"Girl, I've been good. You're looking great," Tori said, taking a seat across from her.

"Thank you. You look like you haven't aged one bit yourself," Andrea replied, admiring Tori's radiant appearance.

"Thank you. You know they say black don't crack," Tori chuckled. "So, what are you doing here?"

SIR JONTONIO

"I just came to get a Frappuccino before I go see my man," Andrea said, taking a sip of her drink.

"Your man? As in, you only have one?" Tori asked, raising an eyebrow playfully.

"Yes, girl, my man. What do you mean, if I only have one?" Andrea said, laughing.

"Now, you know you had multiple guys back in the day. Most of them always spoiled you because they thought they were gonna be the one to get your goodies," Tori reminded her with a mischievous grin.

"Well, that's why I had multiple friends," Andrea said, giggling. "Those little boys weren't about to get any of this. So, I got what I could from them."

"Sounds like you had it all mapped out," Tori said, laughing.

"Well, I learned from the best. You were dating two friends. You played them so bad," Andrea recalled, shaking her head.

"I did it for you. You know how I ride for my sisters. I heard them clowns trying to bet on who would get your goodies first. So, I gamed one up for about two weeks, and then he took me to shoot pool with his crew. When he walked off, I slid my number to his friend and told him not to say anything because I would deny it. And of course, with him being a lame, he complied," Tori said, smirking.

"You are a true savage. You were my shero," Andrea said, laughing.

"Aawww, thank you, but you know I couldn't let nobody play my little sweet church girl," Tori said, both of them bursting into laughter.

"Church girl?" Andrea repeated, wiping tears from her eyes. "So, are you single or is there a special Mr. Somebody?"

"Girl, I'm so single they should put my face on a dollar. Ever since I said nobody was gonna be able to get any more of the good good because I realized that I'm too special to let any and everyone get a taste of this sweetness. Why, what's up?" Tori said.

FOOL'S GOLD

"Well, I'm talking to this guy, and I really like him, but I don't think he feels the same way about me," Andrea confided, her tone turning serious.

"What? Why don't you think he feels the same way about you? How long have y'all been talking?" Tori asked, leaning in closer.

"We've been talking for a few months, and he is a great guy. I even asked him to meet my parents. Girl, he is so sweet and so funny. He shows me things that I never would have thought to take the time to see. I don't know why he won't meet my parents," Andrea said, frustration creeping into her voice.

"That's odd that he doesn't want to meet your parents. But he sounds like a great guy, and I know he has to be someone special if you're talking about bringing him home. Okay, sis, I see you. So, have you met his parents?" Tori asked.

"No, to be honest, he really doesn't talk about his parents. But I was wondering if you will do me a favor," Andrea said cautiously.

"What is it? 'Cause you be off the wall sometimes," Tori said, eyeing her suspiciously.

"I have a friend coming in from out of town for the weekend, and I was wondering if you could go to this bachelor party for me and see if my man will be faithful to me and isn't checking for any other girls. I know he is going to have fun and do guy things, but I just want to make sure he doesn't cross any lines. My friend is a friend of the family, and I haven't seen her in a while. So, will you do it for me?" Andrea asked, her eyes pleading.

"Sure, when is it? I guess I'll be going to two bachelor parties," Tori said, smiling.

"Two? When is the one you have to go to?" Andrea asked, surprised.

"Friday," Tori replied.

"That's crazy. So is the one I'm asking you to go to for me. The party I'm asking you to go to is for a guy named Zeke," Andrea said.

SIR JONTONIO

"That's crazy. That's the one I'm going to. He's my roommate's cousin. How do you know him?" Tori asked, her eyebrows shooting up.

"That's my man's best friend and he is the best man," Andrea explained.

"Well, girl, you know I got you. What's his name?" Tori asked.

"Antonio, but people call him Tonio. Thank you, girl. Well, I gotta go. I'll text you later, okay? Bye, girl," Andrea said, standing up.

"Okay. Bye, sis," Tori said, waving as Andrea walked out.

As she stepped outside, Andrea called Antonio. "Hey, babe, are you still coming to meet my parents this weekend?" Andrea asked, her voice hopeful.

"Yes, babe, you know I will be there. But I'll talk to you later; I'm getting stuff ready for this wedding," Antonio replied.

"Okay, talk to you later. Love you."

"Love you too," Antonio said before hanging up.

Next, Andrea dialed Jacob's number. "Hey darling, are you ready for this weekend?" she asked.

"You know that I'm excited to get back to my future wifey," Jacob said, his voice warm.

"Well, I was just checking in to see what you were doing."

"Just finishing up some work. I can't wait to see you," Jacob replied.

"Thank you, bae. I will see you this weekend. I love you. I gotta go," Andrea said, smiling.

"I love you too. Bye, bae," Jacob said.

As she hung up the phone, Andrea felt a surge of excitement. She had secured Tori's help, and now she could look forward to the weekend with Jacob, and soon, the introduction of Antonio to her parents. Everything seemed to be falling into place, and she felt grateful for the support and love from her friends and significant others.

As Andrea walked to her car, a gentle breeze carrying the scent of fresh coffee and blooming flowers, she couldn't help but feel hopeful. Life can be complicated, but with a little help from her friends and loved ones, she could navigate anything. And as she drove off, she knew that no matter what, she would always be her sister's keeper.

Chapter 14

Unexpected Connections

Brandon and Zeke strolled through the bustling halls of the mall, surrounded by the buzz of shoppers and the occasional waft of pretzel and cinnamon roll scents. Brandon looked anxiously at his watch, tapping his foot impatiently.

"Yo, have you heard from Tonio?" Brandon asked, scanning the crowd for any sign of their friend.

"No, why?" Zeke responded casually.

"He said he was gonna meet us here 30 minutes ago. I don't have all day. You know today is my girl's birthday and I still got to get her a gift," Brandon sighed, frustration evident in his voice.

"Oh, yeah, that's right. Dang, y'all have been dating for a minute now. You must be in love," Zeke teased, a grin spreading across his face.

"Yeah, we have, and that's my baby. I want to get her a real nice gift, bro," Brandon admitted, a sincere look in his eyes.

"Alright, I got you. Well, let's start looking for a gift until Tonio gets here," Zeke suggested.

"Bet. So, let's hit up Victoria's Secret. My baby likes the lotion from there," Brandon said, leading the way.

Laughing, Zeke replied, "Lotion? I know you lying. You trying to get some lingerie and get her to tell you her secrets, huh?"

"Nah brah, it's not like that. You don't need to be worried about her secrets anyway," Brandon shot back, rolling his eyes.

SIR JONTONIO

Meanwhile, Antonio had just parked his car and started making his way into the mall. As he walked toward the entrance, he noticed a striking woman heading to her car. He hurried his pace to catch up to her.

"Hey, love, excuse me sweetie," Antonio called out, a charming smile on his face.

Andrea turned, her eyes meeting his. "Hey," she replied, intrigued but cautious.

"How are you doing?" Antonio asked, his eyes warm with interest.

"I'm fine," Andrea answered, raising an eyebrow.

"Yes, you are. I see you were leaving, and I couldn't let this opportunity pass me by," Antonio said smoothly, his smile widening.

"Opportunity? What opportunity are you talking about?" Andrea said, crossing her arms.

"Letting you leave without introducing myself and getting your number so I can call you and set up a date so we can get to know each other," Antonio said, his tone earnest.

"That was cute, but I don't know about all of that. I don't give my number out to strangers," Andrea replied skeptically.

"Well, my name is Antonio, and I'm from the View," he said, extending his hand.

"Nice to meet you. I have people from the View," Andrea said, shaking his hand.

"That's what's up. So, what's your name?" Antonio asked.

"My name is Andrea," she replied.

"Drea. That's cute. So, when do you want me to pick you up?" Antonio asked, his eyes sparkling with mischief.

"How you gonna pick me up if you don't have my number?" Andrea teased.

"So, what's your number then?" Antonio asked, leaning in slightly.

FOOL'S GOLD

"That was cute. 757-555-8899. Hit me later because I have to go," Andrea said, handing him a piece of paper with her number scribbled on it.

Antonio finally made his way to the food court, where Brandon and Zeke were waiting for him. They spotted him and waved him over.

"Look who decided to finally show up," Brandon said, a playful smirk on his face.

"Bro, you would definitely be late to your own funeral," Zeke added, shaking his head.

"Shut up. What's good? What all y'all bought?" Antonio asked, taking a seat.

"Just left Victoria's Secret," Zeke said.

"Yeah, today's my girl's birthday and I had to buy her a gift," Brandon explained.

"That's what's up. Have y'all eaten yet?" Antonio inquired.

"No," Brandon replied.

"Nah, we were waiting on you and I'm starving," Zeke said, rubbing his stomach.

As they sat down to figure out what to eat, a familiar face walked up.

"Tonio, is that you?" a woman's voice called out.

Antonio turned to see a stunning woman approaching.

"Who's asking?" he said, squinting to place her.

"I know it's been a while, but don't tell me you forgot about little ole me," she said, her smile broadening.

"Miranda, is that you?" Antonio asked, his face lighting up.

"Yeah, it's me," Miranda replied, her eyes twinkling.

"Dang, you really grew up. You look amazing. How have you been? What are you doing here?" Antonio asked, genuinely happy to see her.

"You look good too. I'm here doing some last-minute shopping for a gift for someone. But I'm in a rush. Take my number and let's set up a dinner date so we can catch up," Miranda suggested, handing him a business card.

SIR JONTONIO

"Sure. That sounds like a plan," Antonio said, pocketing the card.

After Miranda walked away, the trio resumed their mission to find Brandon's girlfriend a perfect gift. They finally decided on a perfume from a luxury store, something Brandon knew she would love.

Later, as the sun began to set and the mall started to wind down, the three friends sat at a table in the food court, bags of purchases at their feet. They laughed and reminisced about old times, the weight of the day's tasks finally lifting.

"Man, today was crazy," Brandon said, leaning back in his chair.

"Yeah, I feel you. But it was worth it," Zeke said, nodding.

Antonio's mind wandered back to Andrea and the unexpected meeting with Miranda. It had been a day of chances and choices, and he couldn't help but feel that something significant was on the horizon.

As they gathered their things to leave, Antonio's phone buzzed with a new message. It was from Andrea: *Looking forward to hearing from you. :)*

He smiled, feeling a sense of anticipation. He had a feeling this was just the beginning of something exciting and new.

"Ready to roll out?" Antonio asked, looking at his friends.

"Yeah, let's go," Brandon and Zeke replied in unison.

They walked out of the mall, the night air cool and refreshing. As they headed to their cars, Antonio couldn't shake the feeling that life was about to get a whole lot more interesting.

Chapter 15

The Test of Loyalty

Antonio, Brandon, and Zeke cruised down the highway, the anticipation of the night ahead filling the car. The shimmering skyline hinted at the vibrant party waiting for them in celebration of Brandon's girlfriend's birthday. The bass from the car's stereo matched their excited pulses. "This party is gonna be lit. I'm just glad I have a woman to go home to unlike y'all," Brandon boasted, a proud smirk on his face. "But maybe, just maybe, y'all will get like me... one day." Antonio and Zeke exchanged a glance before bursting into laughter. "Man, what's so funny?" Brandon demanded; his tone tinged with curiosity. "I wanna laugh too." Zeke recovered first, wiping a tear from his eye. "Bro, no disrespect, but she's from Tidewater Park. That's community property." Brandon's joyful expression faded into confusion. "What do you mean, community property? And what does coming from the park have to do with anything?" Antonio joined in, shaking his head. "Man, don't act like you don't know about them park girls. And yeah, I mean yours too." "Community property meaning she's for everybody," Zeke clarified bluntly. "Man, shut up. You sound real stupid right now," Brandon retorted, defensive. "Alright, bet," Antonio interjected, his voice challenging. "If she's as committed as you think, let's see..." Brandon's resolve hardened. "Alright, I know she's mine. I ain't got nothing to worry about. So, what you got in mind?" Zeke grinned mischievously. "Lemme get in on this, Tonio. If I can get her to kiss me, Brandon, you gotta let me go out with that shorty from the mall. But if she doesn't, you get the satisfaction of knowing she's only yours, and I'll give you a heartfelt apology." "Bet," Brandon and Antonio echoed simultaneously.

As they arrived at the party, Brandon surveyed the bustling scene. "Alright, so where's your girl at? It is her party, after all," Antonio asked. "Chill, man. We just got here. I wanna make sure we all straight on the plan," Brandon replied. "If you get your kiss, Zeke, I'll admit I was wrong. If not, then you better back off, and I don't wanna hear nothing about her reputation again." "Aight, man. I got you. Now go find 'ya girl' and let's get this ball rolling," Zeke urged. Brandon walked over to his girlfriend, Destiny, while Zeke and Antonio positioned themselves to observe from a distance.

After a brief conversation, Brandon kissed her and then walked away, signaling Zeke. Zeke approached Destiny confidently. "Happy Birthday, beautiful," he said, flashing a charming smile. "Thank ya, luv. It just got a lot better now," Destiny responded, her eyes twinkling. "Oh word? And would I just so happen to be the cause behind that?" Zeke teased. "Ha ha... don't flatter yourself, Zeke," Destiny retorted playfully. "I gotchu, ma. I'll leave ya be. I did mean it though. Hope you're enjoying yourself. A beautiful girl always deserves the best on her birthday," Zeke said, stepping back. Destiny, caught off guard by his sudden retreat, reached out and grabbed his arm. "Don't be so sensitive, boy. You know I'm just playing. Now come back here. You may have done a little to make my birthday better." "Just a little? Girl, you know you're lying. I made your whole night, and you know it," Zeke quipped, laughing. Destiny giggled. "Boy, you are too funny. Stop talking and come dance with me, make it even better." Zeke followed her to the dance floor, while Brandon and Antonio watched discreetly from the bar.

"Aight, man, what's happened so far? And you better be sure she can't see us," Brandon said, nervously glancing around. "Relax, you know I know how to pick my spots. We can see her, but she can't see us," Antonio assured him. "Yeah, whatever. Aye, why's she all up on him like that?"

FOOL'S GOLD

Brandon's anxiety was palpable. "You mean like she likes him? Well, it sorta looks like she does," Antonio observed, his tone neutral. "Shut the hell up, man. You ain't funny," Brandon snapped. "Brandon, chill. We all agreed on the bet. You know Zeke is just reading and feeding off the energy she puts out," Antonio reasoned. "I don't care how much game he thinks he has. She's not gonna kiss him. She's playing him because she knows his game," Brandon insisted. "Yeah, well, I hope you're right about that," Antonio said, watching the dance floor warily.

Meanwhile, on the dance floor, Zeke was working his charm. "So, you really think I look beautiful tonight?" Destiny asked, a hint of vulnerability in her voice. "Stop playing, ma. You know you're always beautiful no matter what you're wearing," Zeke responded sincerely. Blushing, Destiny said, "You sure know how to sweet talk a girl, don't you?" "Like I said, I'm just being honest, Destiny. Brandon is a really lucky man," Zeke said, his eyes softening. "Well, what if I said I don't feel like the lucky one... that I want to be with someone who makes me feel that way?" Destiny's tone was earnest, almost wistful. "Whatchu mean, girl? You got Brandon's whole heart in your hand. That man will do anything you ask," Zeke said, genuinely surprised. "You say that, but I don't always feel that way. I haven't felt that way for a while, actually," Destiny admitted, her gaze dropping to the floor. "I'm sorry to hear that, ma. You deserve the world. And it's your man's job to give that to you," Zeke said softly. "Well, I think I might have found the man who can give that to me," Destiny said, looking up at Zeke. "Oh, really? And who might that be?" Zeke asked, a playful smile tugging at his lips. Instead of answering, Destiny leaned in and kissed Zeke.

From across the room, Brandon and Antonio watched in shock. Brandon stood abruptly, but Antonio grabbed his arm. "Man, move," Brandon demanded, his anger barely contained. "Nah, where are you going?" Antonio asked, holding him back. "I'm going to thank my bro for doing me a solid. Should have trusted momma when she told me I couldn't turn no hoe into a housewife," Brandon said, his voice harsh.

SIR JONTONIO

Brandon walked over to Zeke and Destiny, causing her to pull back abruptly. He went to dap Zeke. "You helped me dodge a bullet, bro. Honestly, thank you," Brandon said. "No problem, bro. Now where's Tonio? A bet's a bet," Zeke replied, smiling. Brandon pointed out Antonio, who waved and smiled at the trio. Zeke flashed a final grin at both Brandon and Destiny before heading over to Antonio. "What are you talking about, a bet? What the hell is going on, Brandon?" Destiny asked, her voice rising with confusion and hurt. "I know you ain't acting mad, not when you're the one out here cheating," Brandon shot back, his voice cold. Stammering, Destiny said, "No. I-I would never... Brandon, baby, let me explain. You don't know what you saw." "Nah, I know exactly what I saw. Man, I should have known better. All y'all girls from out the park are the same," Brandon said, his disappointment clear. Trying not to cry, Destiny said, "No, we are not. No, I am not. Baby, please." "Nah, Destiny. I see you now. I mean I actually see YOU. I can't get back the year that I already wasted, and I'll be damned if I waste another second in your presence," Brandon said, his voice final. He turned and walked back to the bar, drowning his sorrows. Destiny stood there, upset and crying, before fleeing the room.

Meanwhile, Antonio had given Zeke Miranda's number as promised and was looking for Brandon. Andrea, Destiny's friend, entered the party and started to look for her. Antonio spotted her and made his way over. "You know, when you said we would link up, I didn't expect that to mean you'd be stalking me," he said, trying to lighten the mood. Andrea laughed. "Boy, ain't nobody stalking you. I'm here looking for somebody," she replied. "Right. And the name ain't 'boy,' luv. It's Antonio," he corrected with a grin. "I know your name, Tonio. Do you even remember mine?" Andrea asked, teasingly. "Of course, I do, Andrea. A lovely name that belongs to an even lovelier girl," Antonio said smoothly. "Well, aren't you smooth, Antonio. And what are you doing here?" Andrea asked, intrigued. "Just here with some friends. But why talk about that when I can get to know you?" Antonio responded. "And what do you wanna know about me?" Andrea asked, curiosity piqued. "Anything you're willing to share. You're something different, ma. I see that, and I would like to see even more," Antonio said, his eyes sincere. "Well, how about you buy me a drink, and then we can go somewhere more private? That way we can get to know each other without being distracted," Andrea suggested, her smile inviting. Antonio grinned, leading her to the bar. The night was far from over, and new possibilities were just beginning to unfold.

Chapter 16

Skeletons

Text Messages

Tori's heart hammered in her chest as she typed furiously on her phone. She sent Andrea a message: "We need to talk." The silence from Andrea's end was deafening. Frustrated, she sent another text, "Well, since you're busy, I guess I'll just text you. Look, I love you and all, but I can't continue to lie to Antonio. I know that I was supposed to keep tabs on him, but he is a good man. Nah, scratch that—he's a great man and he deserves to know the truth. You know you are like a sister to me, and I would never do anything to hurt you. When we first met and you told me to make sure he doesn't cheat on you, I was locked in because I thought all men were dogs and didn't think that there were any good men left. After spending time with Tonio, I got to see his heart and how his mind works. Never thought I would fall for someone again after the hurt I experienced in the past. In this short period, Antonio has been like a breath of fresh air, and I feel like I have a clean slate, and I'm not afraid to love someone or be loved by someone. Look, all I'm saying is that you have someone who is special, and I can't lie anymore because I don't want to hurt him. I truly care about him and his well-being. I'm heading over to his place in a few, and I'm going to come clean about everything. Hopefully, he can forgive me and understand that I was just trying to look out for my sister. I love you, Drea, and I'm sorry."

Honeymoon Preparations

Zeke and Miranda were in the midst of packing for their honeymoon. The excitement was palpable as they tucked away swimsuits and passports. Miranda was giddy, "Oh my gosh... we are actually married."

"I know, right? Can't believe I married the love of my life," Zeke replied, his eyes sparkling with happiness.

"Are you excited to go to Fiji and Greenland?" Miranda asked, grinning.

"I'm excited to get them draws," Zeke teased with a playful smirk.

"Why are you so nasty?" Miranda giggled, swatting at him.

"I'm not nasty, bae. I'm just playing. Yes, I am excited to travel with you. This is my first time going out of the states. Now come on before we are late," Zeke responded, grabbing a suitcase.

"Ok, bae," Miranda said. She picked up her phone and noticed a missed call and several voicemails. Listening to the messages, her heart dropped as she learned that the child, she had given up for adoption wanted to meet the biological parents. Overcome with emotion, she texted the biological father quickly. Zeke noticed her distress when he walked in.

"Bae, what's wrong?"

"Nothing," she said, looking at her ring. "Just excited to be married to my Superman, who is my best friend and love of my life."

"That's sweet, bae, but come on before we miss our flight," Zeke urged.

"Coming, bae," Miranda said, forcing a smile.

Antonio's Dilemma

Antonio paced back and forth, clutching his phone. His mind was awash with thoughts as he texted Tori. "Hey, are you busy? I would love to see you. You've been on my mind, and I want to spend time with you."

Tori texted back almost immediately. "Hey sweetheart, I was just thinking of you and was about to text you. That's so sweet of you. I would love to see you too. I have to make a few stops then I'll be on my way."

FOOL'S GOLD

Feeling conflicted, Antonio texted back, "Bet. I'll see you soon." He sat on the couch, lost in contemplation. His feelings for Tori were complex. She made him feel things he'd sworn never to feel again. With Tori, he felt appreciated, seen, and needed. She made him feel like the greatest version of himself, whereas Andrea made him feel pressured to conform to an ideal.

"On one hand, Tori makes me feel things I thought I would never feel again. She makes me want to open up and give God a chance again. I can be myself with her, flaws and all. On the other hand, Andrea is cool, but it seems like she's been distant and hiding something. Andrea puts this pressure on me to be who she wants me to be, not who I truly am. Sometimes I feel like she only wants me because we come from different worlds." A knock interrupted his thoughts.

Antonio yelled, "Who is it?"

A soft voice responded, "Daddy, it's me. Come open the door."

Surprise Visit

In shock, Antonio opened the door to find Andrea standing there, drenched from the rain. "What are you doing here?"

"I came to see you because I missed you and wanted to give you something," Andrea explained.

"I missed you too, but why didn't you just call instead of coming out here in the storm?" Antonio asked.

"Because I wanted to see you face to face and spend time with you. Are you going to invite me in or nah?" Andrea teased.

"Yea, come in," Antonio insisted. "So, what do you have to give me if your hands are empty?"

Andrea walked Antonio over to the couch, pushed him down, and said, "I've been thinking about this for a while now, and I really care about you. I want to take our relationship to the next level." As she spoke, she opened up her trench coat to reveal lingerie, leaving Antonio stunned.

SIR JONTONIO

"What are you doing? I thought you wanted to save yourself for marriage," Antonio stammered.

"I did, but I know that I love you, and I want to spend the rest of my life with you, so why wait?" Andrea replied. She began to undress him as she kissed him.

Trying to keep his composure, Antonio said, "Drea, we need to talk."

"We can talk later. Right now, I just want you to make love to me," Andrea insisted.

"Are you sure?" Antonio asked, his voice wavering.

"Yes, Daddy, I'm sure. Make love to me right here, because baby, it's yours and I can't fight it anymore," Andrea whispered passionately. Not knowing that the door was still ajar, Antonio picked Andrea up and took her to the bedroom, closing the door behind them.

Tori's Heartbreak

Nervous about confessing everything, Tori approached Antonio's house. Seeing the door slightly open, she assumed he'd left it open for her. She stepped inside and found a soaking wet trench coat with high heels tossed on the floor. As she ventured deeper inside, she heard unmistakable sounds of intimacy. Following the trail of discarded clothes, she reached the bedroom door and heard Andrea moaning, "Yes, Tonio, just like that. I love you, Daddy," followed by Antonio's reply, "I love you too, Drea."

Heartbroken, Tori's eyes filled with tears. She stormed out of Antonio's house, rushed to her car, and sped off, crying in the storm.

TO BE CONTINUED!!!

Don't miss out!

Visit the website below and you can sign up to receive emails whenever Sir JonTonio publishes a new book. There's no charge and no obligation.

https://books2read.com/r/B-A-UTTSB-BZDQD

BOOKS 2 READ

Connecting independent readers to independent writers.

About the Author

Hailing from New Orleans, Louisiana, Sir JonTonio is a multifaceted talent: a father, son, brother, actor, scriptwriter, videographer, podcaster, and now, author. Deeply rooted in his love for God, Sir JonTonio is excited to share his first literary work with the world. Having dedicated significant time to this project, he feels the moment has come to unveil what he has been passionately crafting. He hopes that "Fool's Gold" will inspire readers and act as a catalyst, encouraging people globally to pursue their dreams and never give up. Laissez les bons temps rouler!